Yes
I Can!

*To the children who inspire us with their confidence
and resilience despite adversity—KB, JT, & CF*

*For Marianne and Roy Myler, the best parents
any kid could hope to have—VL*

American Psychological Association
750 First Street NE
Washington, DC 20002

Magination Press is a registered trademark of the American Psychological Association.
Order books here: www.apa.org/pubs/magination or 1-800-374-2721

Book design by Sandra Kimbell
Printed by Lake Book Manufacturing, Inc., Melrose Park, IL

Library of Congress Cataloging-in-Publication Data

Names: Barrett, Kendra J., author. | Toner, Jacqueline B., author. |
Freeland, Claire A. B., author. | Lemay, Violet, illustrator.
Title: Yes I can! : a girl and her wheelchair / by Kendra J. Barrett, DPT,
Jacqueline B. Toner, Ph.D., & Claire A.B. Freeland, Ph.D. ;
illustrated by Violet Lemay.
Description: Washington, DC : Magination Press, [2018] | "American
Psychological Association." | Summary: "Carolyn is in a wheelchair, but
she doesn't let that stop her! She can do almost everything the other kids
can, even if sometimes she has to do it a little differently"— Provided by publisher.
Identifiers: LCCN 2017058188| ISBN 9781433828690 (hardcover) |
ISBN 1433828693 (hardcover)
Subjects: | CYAC: People with disabilities—Fiction. |
Individuality—Fiction. | Self-confidence—Fiction. | Ability—Fiction. |
Schools—Fiction. | Friendship—Fiction. | Family life—Fiction.
Classification: LCC PZ7.1.B37265 Yes 2018 |
DDC [E]—dc23 LC record available at https://lccn.loc.gov/2017058188

Manufactured in the United States of America
10 9 8 7 6 5 4 3 2 1

Yes I Can!

A Girl and Her Wheelchair

by Kendra J. Barrett, DPT,
Jacqueline B. Toner, PhD,
and Claire A. B. Freeland, PhD

illustrated by Violet Lemay

Magination Press • Washington, DC
American Psychological Association

This is Carolyn.
Like many kids her age, Carolyn loves animals, castles, and building with blocks.

She is helpful to her mom and dad and even to her baby brother.

Carolyn started a new school this year. She thinks her teacher seems nice and she is getting to know her classmates. The other students are curious about Carolyn because she uses a wheelchair.

When she was born, her body did not work like most people's. She cannot use her legs to walk. But she can do almost everything at school, even when she needs to do things a bit differently.

She joins right in during reading time. The teacher asks if the children can think of words that rhyme with "cat."

Carolyn says, "Yes I can!" She is excited to add to the list.

rat
bat
sat
mat

Hat!

Pat!

Splat!

Sometimes Carolyn can do what the other kids do with just a little help.

At circle time, Carolyn wants to sit on the carpet with her classmates. Her teacher helps her get out of the wheelchair. When her teacher asks if she can come up front to help with the morning song, Carolyn says, "Yes I can!"

Instead of walking, Carolyn uses her hands to scoot on her bottom to get to the front of the class. The first few times the other students stared because they had never seen a kid move like this, but now they're used to it and they hardly notice.

When the students return to their desks, the teacher asks, "Who would like to feed Toffee?" Carolyn raises her hand up high, but the teacher picks Jack to feed the class bunny.

She says, "Carolyn, you can hand out these papers to the class." It's hard to fit her wheelchair between the desks and chairs, and it's frustrating, but Carolyn says, *"Yes I can!"*

At lunch time, Aamira asks if Carolyn can eat with her.
Carolyn says, "Yes I can!"

Carolyn and Aamira travel in line with their class to the
cafeteria. Carolyn pulls her wheelchair up to the lunch table.
Aamira sits on the end so that Carolyn can sit right next to her!
Carolyn shares the cookies she baked at home with her dad.

Today is a super fun day because Carolyn's class is taking a field trip to a bowling alley! Sarah asks if Carolyn can ride the bus with them. Carolyn says, "Yes I can!"

Carolyn's teacher has a special bus come. Carolyn gets to ride up on a rear elevator made just for wheelchairs!

At the bowling alley, Justin asks if Carolyn can bowl.
Carolyn says, "Yes I can!"

Carolyn asks Justin to help set up a ramp at the end of the
lane. She needs someone to lift the heavy ball to the top of
the ramp, but then she can push the ball down the alley.
Everyone in the class wants a turn using the ramp!

One of Carolyn's new school friends, Jasmine, invites all the classmates to her birthday party on Saturday.

Carolyn's mother tells her that the party is at a trampoline gym. "You won't be able to join the other kids in jumping, but you can go to the party and watch." Carolyn says, "Yes, I could."

The other kids are having so much fun on the trampolines that they hardly talk to Carolyn. She's feeling pretty sad and lonely and thinking maybe she should have stayed at home.

Then Jasmine's aunt walks in with Jasmine's little cousin, Tina.
Tina is about the same age as Carolyn's brother, and Carolyn knows
that babies love playing peek-a-boo. Since she's feeling pretty bored,
Carolyn starts to play with the baby.

Soon baby Tina begins laughing. Two girls leave the trampoline
and come over to play with the baby too.

At home, after the party, Carolyn tells her mom how she felt left out at first but that, in the end, she was glad she went.

Her mom tells Carolyn that she's proud of her for finding ways to have a good time even though there are things she can't do. "That's okay," says Carolyn. "There's a lot I can do, and my new friends are really great!"

The next day at recess, the kids are having a running race. A boy from another class calls out, "She can't run so she can't play!"

Carolyn feels sad and left out. She says, "I don't know how I can."

Jimmy says, "Yes you can! Carolyn, you can be the referee. That's an important job because you get to announce who wins each race!"

Carolyn is glad when she can be a part of things,
even if she can't do everything the other kids can.

That night, Carolyn tells her dad how Jimmy helped her to join in with the others.

"Well, Carolyn, I'm glad your new friends can find ways to help you play with them."

Carolyn says, *"Yes, they can!"*

Note to Parents, Caregivers, and Teachers

One of the many jobs of adults who are raising children is fostering an attitude of kindness towards others. We teach respect, inclusion, fairness, and positive communication so that our children build their social skills and get along with their peers. You can teach your children to learn about and be a friend to children who have disabilities as well. This book will give you the information and the skills to do so. For a child in a wheelchair, this book offers a way to talk about their needs for accommodation in the context of a heroine who is appealing and socially successful.

We tell the story of Carolyn, a first-grade student who is in a wheelchair. Of course, there are many reasons for a young child to be in a wheelchair and many different sorts of problems they face. In our story, Carolyn is bright and aware. She is a friendly child who seeks opportunities to socialize.

When children who require wheelchairs first enter school, their peers may be confused and cautious about approaching them. This can result in the child with a disability becoming isolated and their classmates feeling awkward and failing to learn important lessons about interacting with others with differences.

Classmates may be more willing to reach out to a child in a wheelchair when they have a modest amount of adult support and when open discussion is encouraged. Kids often have a lot of questions when they first interact with someone with a disability and, though parents and teachers want to be straightforward in their answers, it can sometimes be hard to know what to say. It's important to emphasize that a classmate in a wheelchair can do most everything other children can do as long as they have assistance and adaptations. Here are some questions children may have about Carolyn, as well as some suggested answers:

What is a disability?
If someone has a disability, it means they aren't able to do some things the same way most people do them. Some people use a wheelchair if a part of their body doesn't work. Because they can't walk, they need a wheelchair to help them get around. Others might use crutches or even have a service dog to help them.

How does someone get a disability?
For many people, a disability is something they are born with. In Carolyn's case, her spine didn't grow normally. Others may have a disability because they had an accident or an illness.

Will I get a disability like Carolyn's?
It's not likely. Carolyn's disability happened before she was even born.

❓ How long will she be in a wheelchair? Will she get better?

Many kids who use a wheelchair will be in the wheelchair forever. As she grows bigger, Carolyn will get bigger wheelchairs that fit her.

❓ How does she eat?

Carolyn eats just like you and I do!

❓ How does she use the bathroom?

Some kids can go to the bathroom normally, but some kids in wheelchairs can't feel when they need to go to the bathroom. In Carolyn's case, she wears a diaper. A grown-up checks her every day on a schedule to see if she needs a diaper change.

❓ Does Carolyn sleep in her wheelchair?

No, Carolyn sleeps in a bed just like you do. Carolyn can move from her wheelchair into her bed all by herself. Her mom and dad have to change her diaper and help Carolyn put on her pajamas, then they tell her a story and kiss her good night.

❓ What will Carolyn be when she grows up?

Whatever she wants to be! She is smart and friendly just like you!

❓ Does Carolyn need extra help during her school day?

Yes. Carolyn has special teachers and therapists who help her during the day. Her special teachers help her with her school work. Her physical therapist helps her learn how to use her wheelchair, how to move around on the floor, and how to get in and out of her wheelchair.

❓ What does she play with at home?

She plays with toys and dolls at home. She plays computer games and she loves to go outside and play with her friends. She loves to play catch—she throws a baseball from her wheelchair. She can play with whatever she wants!

❓ Where can she go?

She can go anywhere that a wheelchair can go: the zoo, the movies, the park, the mall, the aquarium, an ice cream parlor, a restaurant, the arcade, the library, and other places, too. Of course, there are some places that Carolyn isn't able to go to easily. If there are lots of stairs or there is uneven ground, her wheelchair won't help her. Sometimes an adult can carry her into a building without a ramp, or across a field, but not always. That can make Carolyn feel sad, frustrated, angry, or left out.

❓ Can she come to my house?

If there are stairs to get into your house, it might be difficult for her to come over. If she can't come over, she can meet you at a fun place!

❓ How does she ride in the car?

If she has a special car, she can stay in her wheelchair while riding in the car. Otherwise, a grown-up will help put her in a regular seat or a booster seat.

❓ How does she ride on the bus?

She can stay in her wheelchair while riding the school bus. She uses a lift, like an elevator, to go into the bus.

❓ Do her family members use wheelchairs?

No, they can walk. In families, different people have different challenges.

❓ Is she sad to be in a wheelchair?

Carolyn sometimes feels sad and sometimes feels happy, just like you! Sometimes she might feel sad if her friends are doing something that she can't do, like climbing a jungle gym. She feels happy when other kids are playing games she can be a part of.

❓ Can I have a turn in the wheelchair?

No. A wheelchair is just for the person who uses it. It might seem fun like a bicycle, but a wheelchair is not a toy. It's very special and needs to be treated with care.

Sometimes, even with answers to questions, some children continue to be reluctant to interact with a classmate with a disability. Encourage your children to smile and say hello. If you are a parent or caregiver, reach out to the parent of the child who uses a wheelchair and suggest a play date. Talk to your child about their reluctance. Help them put their worries into words. It can be easier to address specific worries or questions, like we did above, than an unspecified reluctance.

If you are reading this book because your child has teased or made fun of a classmate with a disability, remind them that all children have feelings and that their classmate feels hurt just like your child would if someone teased them. Model kindness toward people with disabilities.

Demonstrate making eye contact with and saying hello to people in wheelchairs.

With some basic information, and adjusting games and activities so that a peer with a disability can participate, young children can easily learn to make accommodations for peers with disabilities. If you are fortunate enough to guide children in this process, they may surprise you with their motivation and creativity. The experience of working together to solve problems of playing with one another can allow a child in a wheelchair to feel included and provide a learning experience in empathy for classmates.

About the Authors

Kendra J. Barrett, DPT, is a pediatric physical therapist who has worked in early intervention and public schools for eight years since graduating from Ithaca College with a doctorate in physical therapy. She currently works in a public school for students age 3-21 with intellectual and physical disabilities. This is her first book, and she was thrilled to work with her mom on this project. Dr. Barrett lives in Towson, MD, with her husband, and she welcomed her first child, a boy, during the process of writing this book.

Jacqueline B. Toner, PhD, is the co-author of a number of books for children and teens addressing social and emotional challenges. She practiced clinical psychology for over three decades serving children, teens, and families. Dr. Toner lives in Baltimore, MD, with her husband. They have three married daughters and two grandsons. It has been a special joy to co-write this book with her second born!

Claire A. B. Freeland, PhD, is a clinical psychologist in private practice, working for more than thirty-five years with youth and their families. With an interest in bringing psychological concepts to a wide audience, she has co-written several books for children and teens on subjects related to emotions and behavior. She lives with her husband in Baltimore, MD. They have two grown children.

About the Illustrator

Violet Lemay was a stage designer, a college art professor, and an editorial illustrator before arriving at her dream job: illustrating books for kids. Violet has illustrated over twenty books, a handful of which she also wrote. If she's not at her desk drawing, she's probably in the backyard feeding the birds, who think she is Snow White.

About Magination Press

Magination Press is an imprint of the American Psychological Association, the largest scientific and professional organization representing psychologists in the United States and the largest association of psychologists worldwide.